For Jil

A memorable student, an outstanding parent... I have

# *9 Lives, I Will Survive*

full confidence that you are also an excellent educator.

## By

I am so proud of you

## Jan Crossen

and honored to reconnect

**A fictional story inspired by my son, Joshua.**

with you. Remember — miracles happen.

All the best —

Jan Crossen

Dragonpublishing.net
Illinois

Hall Pass —

Published by
Dragonpublishing.net
www.dragonpublishing.net
Illinois

First printing.

Cover design by Shelley Baar

ISBN-13: 978-0-9793981-9-3
ISBN-10: 0-9793981-9-3

Printed in the United States of America

# Dedications

This book is dedicated to my son, Josh. I admire your courage and tenacious spirit. You've made my life rich with experiences and I love you very much.

To my life partner, Honey B, thank you for your continuous love, strength and support. I know that I am happiest when we are together.

In loving memory of my Baby Sister, Jill, who defined the word "mother," and was my inspiration to become one.

With deep love and gratitude, to my parents, John and Aldine, who taught me the love of family. Thank you for the many blessings in my life.

To my sisters, Jonadine and Jill, I am honored to call you my sisters. I pick each of you, to be my sister next time around too, and I still want to be in the middle.

To Jill's family, her husband Michael, and their children Rob, Chelsey, and Zachary, thank you for your love and support. 'Love Lu.'

I'd like to thank my wonderful extended family; my aunts, uncles, cousins and friends for making my family feel welcome and accepted. You are fantastic and I love you all very much.

To my 'sister-in-law' Linda, thank you for your unconditional love and support. In loving memory of Bob and Nadine, who always made me feel part of the family. To Uncle Bill and Aunt Marian, I appreciate your welcoming Josh and me into the fold.

To Jerri and Paul, Connie and Bonnie, and Joan, thank you so much for your love and support.

To Katy and Doug, thanks for your friendship and for always bringing a smile to my face or a tear to my eye with your music. You're simply the best.

To all families created through adoption and to all of the parents and families with children who are victims of

Fetal Alcohol Spectrum Disorders. We know that it takes a village of support to raise our special children. Blessed be.

# Acknowledgements

Thank you, Josh, for inspiring this book, and for allowing me to utilize experiences from your own story, in the making of this book series.

Honey B, thank you, for helping and sustaining me during this process and throughout our years together. You feed my heart, mind, spirit, and soul. You've given me a permanent smile and made mine the happiest stomach on the island.

To Joshua's birth father, Reginald, thank you for never giving up on finding our boy; and for being there for him now, as he continues his journey into manhood. Together we make a strong circle of support for our Joshua.

Thanks to LeJana and her family for all that they have done for Joshua. A special thanks to Jason for pulling him up from the bottom of the pool.

Thank you to St. Nicholas Adoptions in Tucson, AZ; to our case workers, Christy and Vicky, and to the many social workers, therapists, doctors, EMTs, respite caregivers and teachers whose time, knowledge, guidance, and expertise have helped Josh throughout the years.

Thank you, Teresa Kellerman, of the Fetal Alcohol Syndrome Community Resource Center, in Tucson, AZ for sharing your knowledge and experiences with so many families, and for your belief in this project.

To my long time pal and humor writer, Peg Murphy, thank you for your encouragement and guidance in getting this story into print, and for your e-mails that made me smile.

Thank you, Steve Cox, for your help and editing suggestions for this book.

My heartfelt thanks to the folks at Dragonpublishing.net, and especially to Paul, for his patience and hard work to get this first book, of the *9Lives* series, into print.

# A Note From the Author

The *9 Lives* book series is fictional but was inspired by my son, Joshua. The behaviors and experiences are typical of someone affected by Fetal Alcohol Spectrum Disorders.

My goals for writing these books are:

- to raise awareness of Fetal Alcohol Spectrum Disorders, especially the 'Invisible Disorder' known as Alcohol Related Neurological Disorder (ARND) formerly known as Fetal Alcohol Effect (FAE).
- to write books for teens and adults with FASD.
- to write books for those with low reading abilities.
- to write books for children and teens in foster care.
- to write books for children and teens who have been adopted.
- to write books for children and teens living in interracial homes.
- to write books for children and teens living with same sex parents.

I hope that you enjoy the *9 Lives* series, and that you will share these books with others. Please tell the girls, teens, and women in your life that no amount of alcohol is safe to consume when a woman is expecting a baby.

Fetal Alcohol Spectrum Disorders are preventable birth defects. If you would like to promote healthy births and babies, you can do so by donating to the March of Dimes via their website. www.marchofdimes.com

If you would like to make a contribution in Joshua's name, click on "bandingtogether" and then "Find a Band." Type in "Josh Crossen" and his baby wristband will appear on your screen. You may also create a band in the name of someone that you love, and make a donation that way.

My Joshua was born on 4/14/89 in Tucson, AZ. He was 14 weeks premature and weighed 2 pounds, 2 ounces.

Thank you,
Jan Crossen

"When Jan gave me the manuscript, I sat down and read *9 Lives; I Will Survive,* in one day. I really didn't want to put it down. I was so absorbed in the experiences of this little boy.

**9 Lives, I Will Survive,** was inspired by Jan's own adopted son, and is told from his point of view. This little boy went through so much during his childhood and has to cope with the difficulties of prenatal alcohol exposure.

This touching story has a therapeutic effect. It has the potential to heal the emotional wounds carried by adopted children, birth parents, and adoptive parents.

I would recommend this book for all children, teens, and parents. This book was a joy to read. I will put a copy in the hands of every family that comes through our doors."

Teresa Kellerman, Director,
Fetal Alcohol Syndrome Community Resource Center
Tucson, AZ
www.fasstar.com

# Chapter 1

## *A Time of Innocence*

I've been told that I'm like a cat. People say that cats are lucky because they have nine lives. Somehow, they can survive eight brushes with death. If it's true that I'm like a cat, then I'm eighteen years old and already on life #5. My very existence is a miracle.

This book is about my early years. My life has been pretty amazing so far. I want to share some of my experiences with you.

A lot of wonderful things happened to me too. Like when I was eight years old and first met my mom. That may sound kind of weird to you, but you see, I'm adopted.

My name is Joshua and I'm black. My mom, Jamie Carson, is white. We're an inter-racial family. Mom says that's part of our charm.

Starting at the beginning means that you need to hear about what happened even before I was born. My birth parents are DeShona and Randall Radford Sr. They are both black and were 28 years old when I was born.

My folks had been married two years when I came along. I'm the middle child. My older brother is Randall Jr, or RJ. My baby sister is Amanda. We sometimes called her Mandy.

My family didn't have a lot of money. Dad was a cook and Mom was an aide who took care of old people. Even though they had jobs, it was always a struggle to pay the rent and other bills.

My parents had serious problems and fought a lot. They were not a good match for each other. My parents tried to avoid their pain. Instead of making things better, everything got worse.

My mother was insecure, so she turned to other men to make her feel pretty and wanted. As a result, RJ and Mandy are my half-brother and half-sister. They each have different fathers than I do. My dad is Randall Sr.

DeShona also partied to feel better. She smoked crack and drank alcohol, and it made her really sick. It also made her mean and violent.

My father was living a lie. He was married to my mom, but knew he wasn't the father of two of her children.

And, my dad was attracted to other men. He was afraid that if he came out and told people he was gay, that his family would reject him.

And he was right about that, A few years later, when my dad did come out to his family, they did turn away from him. Man, what's with that?

Dad was messed up on drugs and Mom on drugs and alcohol. They didn't mean to, but they neglected us kids. Things were awful! Lies, drugs, and alcohol broke my birth family apart.

Alcohol damaged RJ, Amanda, and me even before we were born. Mom drank booze while she was pregnant with me.

I'm eighteen now and didn't know about her drinking until four months ago. It sure explains a lot of things. I'll tell you about all of that some other time.

You see, whatever the mother eats or drinks, her baby does too. So if a woman drinks alcohol, smokes cigarettes, or does drugs, so does her fetus. A fetus is another name for a baby before it's born.

Did you know that the fetus gets its food from the mother's blood supply? Can you imagine feeding beer to a baby? Me neither. But that's what happened.

DeShona didn't drink just one beer; she drank two or three six-packs, or a bottle of wine, or a bottle of booze, by herself, in one night. She wasn't fussy about what she drank. She was a sneaky drinker and would hide her liquor. She'd swallow whatever alcohol she could get.

Alcohol causes birth defects and permanent brain damage to the innocent unborn child. And a woman doesn't need to be an alcoholic to hurt her fetus.

It only takes a small amount of liquor to harm a baby for life. No amount of alcohol, not one beer, one glass of wine, or one shot of whiskey, is safe to drink when a woman is pregnant.

13

Because of DeShona's drinking, RJ, Amanda, and I will never reach our full potential. It isn't fair. We were screwed out of a normal life, even before we took our first breaths of air.

# Chapter 2

## *A Time of Consequences*

My dad had just returned home from work and was in the kitchen fixing himself a quick snack, when he heard my mom's frantic screams.

"Randall, help me!" DeShona screamed as she dropped to the bathroom floor. "I'm bleeding, Randall...Randall, where are you? I need you!"

DeShona was pregnant with me. I was a tiny, twenty-six week old fetus, developing in her womb. My mom's placenta was tearing away from the uterine wall. The blood, flowing through her placenta, brought food and oxygen to me. It kept me alive. Right now, I was in grave danger of dying.

"Randall, the blood is just gushing out of me. I'm afraid we'll lose the baby, help me, please!" she shouted as loudly as she could.

"Hold on, DeShona, I've called 911 and an ambulance is on the way. Nothing bad is going to happen to you or our baby," my dad tried to reassure her.

"What about RJ?" DeShona asked about my older brother.

"He's still napping. I'll get him up when the EMTs arrive. Everything's going to be all right. Have faith, Woman." Randall said, kneeling down beside her and reaching for her slender hand. Together they waited anxiously for help to arrive.

Most women carry their babies for between 37-40 weeks. DeShona was only 18 weeks into her pregnancy when she started bleeding heavily. This meant that she had been in danger of losing me for 2 months now. Her doctor was very concerned and ordered her to stay in bed.

DeShona left her bed to go to the bathroom. That's when she discovered how badly she was hemorrhaging. She was losing a lot of blood very quickly.

"The ambulance is here, Honey. You and the baby are in good hands now." my dad assured her. "I'll get RJ and we'll meet you at the hospital."

A taxi cab took Dad and my brother to the hospital. Dad ran down the halls, carrying RJ in his arms. He stopped at the emergency room desk long enough to find out where they had taken my mom.

When my birth mom arrived at the hospital she was immediately examined by a doctor.

"We need to do an emergency C-Section, DeShona," he announced. "If we hope to have any chance of saving this baby's life."

Fifteen minutes later, DeShona was in surgery delivering me by Caesarean or C-Section. That means they cut open her belly, and took me from her uterus. Her physician was desperately trying to save my life.

"It's a boy," the doctor said as he gently lifted me from the womb. "But he's awfully tiny."

He wanted me to breathe, so he slapped me on my bare butt. He needed me to cry. At first I was silent, so he spanked again.

"Come on baby boy; let's hear what you're made of."

"Waaaaaaaaaaaaaaaa, Waaaaaaaaaaaaaaaa!" This time I protested the smack on my tender tush.

Everyone smiled with relief. They knew my crying because it meant that I was alive. The nurse took me and put me on the scale.

"2 pounds, 2 ounces," she said.

Suddenly, the room became strangely quiet.

"He's stopped crying, and he's turning blue."

"Get an oxygen mask on him and take him to NICU."

NICU is where the very sick newborns are kept. NICU stands for Neonatal Intensive Care Unit. Each infant in NICU gets extra special care and attention.

"Let's close up the mother so we can focus on the little guy," the doctor said. He turned his attention back to DeShona and sewed her surgery incision. When he finished, he examined me closely.

"He sure is fragile." The physician said to no one in particular. He took a tape measure and began to measure my

17

body. "He's about as long as a ruler, just a hair over 12 inches from head to toe. I've seen softballs that are bigger than this little fellow's head. And check out these skinny little arms and legs. They're as thick as my index finger. Look here, his whole hand is no bigger than my thumb. This newborn wasn't ready to join the world just yet."

The doctor removed the oxygen mask to see how I would function without it. I struggled to breathe and gasped for air.

"He's still having trouble getting enough air. Let's help him breathe." The doctor said handing me to the nurse who positioned my body for the life-saving procedure.

The doctor inserted a tube in my little mouth and down my narrow throat. Someone hooked me up to a machine called a respirator. It made the oxygen flow in and out of my lungs. It helped keep me alive.

My heart was having problems too. It was beating way too fast. Instead of having a steady pace of 'Lub-dub; lub-dub; lub-dub,' the beats were fast and irregular. The rhythm sounded like a drummer who was showing off during his spotlight solo on stage.

My dad had called his mother, Grandma Jodie, and she had come to the hospital. She was sitting with Dad and RJ when the doctor went to see them.

"Mr. Radford, you and your family need to prepare yourselves for the worst. Your son came very early and isn't fully developed. There's a chance that he won't make it through the night," the physician cautioned my family.

"Have you given him a name?"

"Yes, his name is Joshua," Dad replied as he wiped a tear from his eye. "Joshua Nelson Radford."

"May I see my son now?"

"Not just yet, we'll let you know when it's OK to visit Joshua. The nurses have put him an incubator. He was shivering from the cold, so they are warming him with a special heater."

"Thank you, Doctor, thanks everyone," Dad said to the medical staff that was caring for Mom and me.

"You're welcome, Mr. Radford...Um; there's another thing. Joshua can't suck yet. He needs his mother's breast milk, but he can't take it. He needs to go back to surgery, so we can put a feeding tube in his body," the doctor said. "He needs calories and to gain weight."

"OK, do it," Randall said.

They whisked me back into the surgery and sewed a feeding tube to the inside of my stomach. The tube was used to nourish me for several weeks.

Two hours later a nurse found my father and grandmother in the waiting room. My brother, RJ, was asleep on Grandma Jodie's lap.

"You may visit your son now, Mr. Radford," a nurse told my father. "The sink is over there. Scrub your hands and arms well. Then put on a sterile gown, mask, and cap. Cover your shoes with these slippers."

My father did as he was told, then walked into the neonatal nursery where I lay in a small clear box.

"Why is he so restless? May I hold him?"

The nurses answered his questions. They didn't want me out of my incubator yet.

"You can't hold him yet, but it would be fine if you were to gently stroke him with your fingers, like this." The nurse showed my dad what to do.

Dad hummed a song as he softly brushed my head, arms, back, and legs.

"Daddy loves you, Joshua," he whispered. "You're going to be fine, son. You listen to your papa now, you hear me?"

Dad put his index finger against the palm of my right hand and I curled my fingers around it.

"That's right, son. Take all of the energy you need baby to get strong."

19

Grandma Jodie scrubbed and put on a sterile gown too. She sang soft lullabies to me. My family prayed for me to get better.

For several hours my mom was still in the recovery room. It wasn't until later in the day that she was able to visit me. That's when she learned that I might die. She refused to accept that possibility.

"Hello, beautiful baby boy," DeShona cooed as she laid eyes on me for the first time. "I do believe that you're going to be handsome and look just like your Papa. You've got to be strong, now. I know you can do this. I love you, Baby Joshua."

For weeks my dad, mom, or grandmother would visit me in the hospital. Finally, I was allowed out of my incubator for short periods of time, and they were able to hold and rock me.

About three weeks later the doctor wanted my mother to try to nurse me. "Let's see if Joshua can nurse," he said. "DeShona, please sit down over here and try nursing your son. Your milk would really be very good for him if he's able to take it

"Ouch!" she said. "He bites. Let's use a pump to get my milk. Then bottle feed him."

That's what they did. At last, I could drink my mother's milk. It helped me get better. I continued to develop and get stronger. I stayed in the hospital for two months before the doctor would let me go home.

"You may take Joshua home when you can operate his breathing monitor," The doctor told my parents. "If he stops breathing and the alarm sounds, you need to know what to do to save his life."

My folks listened carefully as the nurse explained the monitor and what to do if I stopped breathing. They learned what to do in an emergency.

I went home with my parents. I was still hooked up to IVs and monitors. Luckily, the alarm never sounded and I continued to breathe on my own.

My entry into this world is the beginning of my cat-like nine lives. One brush with death down, eight to go.

# Chapter 3

## *Two Photographs*

There wasn't much meat on my bones when I finally left the hospital. Gaining weight wasn't easy for me, and I was a small fry for a long time.

As time passed I learned to roll over, sit-up, and crawl, like other infants. RJ is only ten months older than I am, and we played together. We had a lot more fun once I learned to walk, run, and talk. RJ thought it was especially fun to bully and beat up on me.

"RJ, get off of me," I said. "Let me up or I'll tell Dad."

"You'd better not, little brother. Now, give me your cookie, I'm hungry!" he said.

I gave him my cookie, but I wasn't happy. He picked on me a lot until our baby sister came along.

About two years after I was born Amanda May joined our family. She was a cute little thing, and always feisty. I liked having a big brother and baby sister.

My folks were still having problems. They were distracted and not taking good care of us.

One summer evening, my folks really got into it with each other. Dad came home from work to find Mom drunk and sitting on the sofa. It should have been time for our baths, but we hadn't even eaten supper yet. Mom and Dad started screaming and yelling at each other. It sounded like two angry cats in an alley.

Within minutes, their arms were locked around each others heads. Losing their balance, they fell with a thud to the living room floor. The room shook from the force. My mother was just as big and strong as my father. They gasped for breath as they wrestled for control.

Huffing and cussing, they squirmed and rolled. Someone's foot kicked a table lamp. It flew into the air and shattered against the television. Large sharp chunks of glass lay on the blue shag rug.

The fighters moved to the kitchen, slamming the high chair which tipped over. Luckily, Mandy was in her playpen and not her highchair.

Pictures fell off the walls. Their frames lay broken on the gray linoleum floor.

One of our neighbors must have called the police. Within ten minutes, a patrol car arrived at our apartment. The cops had been to our place two other times when my folks' fighting had gone out of control.

The officers realized that it was not safe for us to live with our parents. That night they removed us from their home. RJ was four, I was three, and Amanda was just a baby.

For a couple of weeks we lived in a shelter called Casa De Los Ninos. There were a lot of other kids there. It was a safe house where grown-ups didn't yell or fight. It was the beginning of our lives in foster care.

A year later, a judge decided DeShona could no longer be our mother. A caseworker, from the state of Arizona, asked my father to give up his legal rights to be our dad. She tried to convince him that it would be better for us kids if we were raised by someone who was equipped to care for three small children.

My father and mother separated. Now he was a single parent. He was also a closeted gay man who had a drug problem. My dad felt very alone, frightened, and helpless.

My father was worried about providing the proper care for his children. He was very sad the day that he agreed to turn us over to the state of Arizona. He was no longer my legal parent.

I don't remember much from those early days with my birth family. I do have a couple of photographs that were taken back then.

One is a picture of my mother and us kids at the zoo. We're standing in front of the giraffe area. My birth mom was a tall, slender, and stylish black woman. She was very pretty. Mom had a friendly smile and sparkling eyes. You could tell that she liked posing for the camera. I think I remember having that photo taken. Maybe I've just looked at it so many times that it feels like I remember that day.

"You boys go stand by your momma," my father said. "Now, everybody look this way and smile."

Mom was holding Amanda in her arms. Mandy was a pretty little girl. She wore a fancy red dress, with a matching coat and shoes. She looked so sweet and innocent, and had a big smile on her face.

RJ was standing next to Mom. He was trying to look tough in the snap shot. RJ's a teenager now, and he looks just the same as he did in that picture. RJ is a tank; he's solid and built like a MACK truck. If I were in a fist fight, I'd want to have him on my side.

I was still a skinny little kid. I was standing on a fence rail, looking towards Papa who held the camera. He must have been our family photographer.

I have a picture of my dad too. He's tall and thin like I am. We have the same big old teeth-showing grin. Our ears are similar too. I think Dad's handsome and that we look alike. Maybe when I'm a little older, I'll look just like he does in that picture.

I'm glad I have these two photos. They help me understand my history. Those pictures connect me to my beginnings.

I spent just three short years living with my birth family, and don't have many memories of that time. It feels like it was a lifetime ago, and that it all happened to someone else. That existence was my cat life #2.

# Chapter 4

## *Please Hurry!*

RJ, Amanda, and I needed someplace safe to live. We needed new parents, and to start our lives over. We moved to California to live with some relatives.

"Hi Randall Jr., Joshua, and Amanda," said the small black woman as she knelt down to see us face-to-face. I'm your Aunt Suzette and this is your Uncle Joey. Your uncle here is your mom's big brother."

Shyly we looked into the eyes of these strangers. Aunt Suzette gave us a slight smile. She had a small space between her two front teeth, and seeing that made me smile back at her.

"Call me RJ," my brother said. "And we call her Mandy May." He tossed his head towards our sister.

"We don't have any children of our own, so you're coming to live with us," my aunt said. "That way your parents will get to see you and you'll still be part of our family. Come here now and give your Aunt Suzette a big hug."

RJ and I looked at each other. We didn't know what to think of all of this. Mandy walked right up to our aunt & jumped into her open arms.

"Do these kids have any bags?" Uncle Joey asked the social worker who had taken us to California.

"Just this one," the case worker said indicating the black garbage bag in his left hand. He handed it to my uncle, had them sign a release form, and said a quick goodbye.

Aunt Suzette was really nice to us. She wanted to adopt us, but Uncle Joey drank too much. And he wasn't nice when he drank.

On the night before Halloween, Uncle Joey had been drinking beer and smoking cigarettes all day long. The more he drank, the meaner he got.

Our aunt had spent the day helping us put together our costumes for trick-or-treating. We were excited about dressing up and collecting our loot of goodies the next evening. We were already tucked in bed for the night when the trouble started. Uncle Joey started picking a fight with Aunt Suzette.

They were in the kitchen when he began yelling. His words grew louder and he started to cuss. Uncle Joey picked up a dinner plate and threw it, like a Frisbee, at our aunt.

The edge of the plate smacked into her back and Uncle Joey laughed. He began hurling the rest of our dirty dinner dishes in her direction.

"Grunt, crash...grunt, crash!" We heard our uncle's grunting followed by the shattering of dishes. He threw glasses, plates and bowls, some still filled with food, as hard as he could across the kitchen. They fell in tiny pieces on the floor.

RJ climbed down from his bunk and I sprang to my feet.

"We've got to stop him!" RJ growled. We bolted down the hall to help our aunt. Bright red meat sauce and spaghetti noodles stained the wall behind the kitchen table. Broken glass, forks and spoons decorated the floor.

Uncle Joey's face was puffed up. His eyes were full of hate, and his nostrils flared. The veins in his neck and temples were bulging. Spit sprayed out of his mouth when he screamed.

"Stop, Uncle Joey, stop!" RJ begged.

"Please don't hurt Aunt Suzette," I pleaded, "Please!"

He wouldn't listen.

"You kids better get back in your room now, if you know what's good for you!" he threatened.

He loosened his belt and came after us. RJ and I flew down the hall. We slammed and locked the door to our bedroom. We dove under the bed, our hearts pounding against the bare wooden floor.

"Leave those kids alone, Joe!" Aunt Suzette said.

Once again Uncle Joey focused his attention on his wife. Amanda was awake by now, and hiding under some blankets in our closet. We all tried not to breathe too loudly for fear that he might hear us. We couldn't risk him breaking down our door and venting his anger on the three of us.

I heard him yelling again at my aunt. Thinking it was safe, I crawled out from my hiding spot. Quietly, I tip-toed into the room next door. It was Uncle Joey and Aunt Suzette's bedroom. Carefully, I picked up the telephone, and then eased my way back to my safe spot, under our bunk beds.

Crack...hummmmmmmmmmmmmm    I had a dial tone. Studying the numbers I accurately dialed 9-1-1, Beep, Beep, Beep.

"911 what is your emergency?" The operator asked.

Hugging the phone to my ear, I whispered, "Uncle Joey's crazy mad! He's yelling and throwing things at Aunt Suzette."

"What is your name, son?"

"Joshua, Joshua Radford, ma'am."

"How old are you Joshua?"

"I'm seven years old, ma'am."

"Is anyone else in the house besides you and your aunt and uncle?"

"Yes, my brother RJ and my little sister Mandy. We're hiding in our bedroom, with the door locked," I said.

"Good, Joshua. You stay right there. Stay on the line with me. I'll send for help," the operator said.

"Please hurry, we're really scared." My voice quivered as tears welled up in my eyes.

I told her the address and tightened my grip on the phone. I tried not to cry and prayed that help would come soon. RJ, Amanda, and I strained to hear the sound of the wailing sirens.

Aunt Suzette was sobbing and Uncle Joey was still screaming when the police car crunched to a halt in the gravel in front of the house. I watched the pattern of the blue and red lights as they danced around the walls of our room. Those lights were a very welcome sight.

Boom, Boom, Boom. "Open up, Police!" commanded the men in blue.

Uncle Joey held the stub of a filtered cigarette in his mouth. He clutched a half-empty bottle of beer in his hand. He staggered to the door and turned the brass knob.

"Well, hello, officers," my uncle greeted the cops with a sly smirk on his face. He took a long swig from his brown bottle and tossed it into the yard. The glass shattered as it smashed against a gray concrete wall.

The police entered the house. Using calm voices, with respectful words, they began talking with my uncle. He began to calm down.

"I need you to turn around, sir, and put your hands behind your back," a cop said to my uncle.

Uncle Joey did as he was told. The police locked the cuffs around his wrists. They drove him away in their black and white cruiser. Not until then, did I believe that we were truly safe.

"RJ, Josh, Mandy, are you kids all right?" Our aunt called for us.

We ran to her and cried as she rocked us in her arms. We dried our tears and snotty noses on the sleeves of her pink Mickey Mouse sweatshirt.

It was clear to everyone that living with my uncle wasn't safe. This wasn't the first time he had been mean to Aunt Suzette or us. It wasn't our only telephone call for help. But tonight would be the last.

The police told the Department of Children and Families, DCF, about us. The next day a nice lady, driving an old red Volkswagen bug, came to talk with Aunt Suzette.

She told the social worker about our uncle's drinking and his nasty temper. Aunt Suzette admitted that he beat us with his belt. He even whipped the leather across her bare back at least two times. Our aunt said that she was powerless to stop him.

One at a time, the DCF lady asked RJ, Amanda, and me what our uncle had done to us. He hurt me, and I didn't

31

want to talk about it. I started crying when it was my turn to meet with the lady.

"Joshua, I know that your uncle hurt you with his belt. Did he hurt you in any other way?" she asked.

"I don't want to talk about it." I said defiantly and turned my back to the stranger.

"Honey, you didn't do anything wrong. We need to stop your uncle from hurting you or anybody else ever again. Josh, you can trust me. I need to know what your uncle did to you."

"He touched me down there," I said.

"Did your uncle touch your private parts?" she asked.

Keeping my face away from hers I nodded. With the back of my hand, I wiped the tears off my cheeks.

"Oh, sweetheart," she said, "I'm so sorry. What your uncle did to you was wrong. It wasn't your fault," she explained. "He'll never hurt you again, I promise."

The next day the DCF lady took me to some kind of a doctor. The doctor talked with me and we played with some puppets. Then he told the case worker that I was telling the truth.

About four months ago I learned that my Aunt and Uncle had split up. It's better this way. I hope Uncle Joey has stopped drinking and smoking. I pray Aunt Suzette isn't afraid of him any more. To this day, I hate the smell of beer and cigarettes. It reminds me of Uncle Joey and that terrible night.

Living through hell with Uncle Joey is my third cat life. That's three lives down, and I was only seven years old.

# Chapter 5

## *The Owens Family*

That was the last time that RJ, Amanda, and I lived together. The social worker couldn't find a home that would take all three of us, so we had to split up.

"Give your brother and sister a hug," the case worker said. "You're all going to be living with different families now, so say good-bye and tell them you love them."

I did as I was told, then burst into tears.

"No, no, don't leave me," I screamed as RJ and Amanda were escorted into two different cars. "I want RJ and Mandy," I sobbed, my heart broken. My small body shook with grief at our separation from one another.

"It's going to be all right, Joshua," the adoption worker tried to comfort me. "Amanda already has two new wonderful parents who will love and adore her. She'll be just fine, and so will you and Randall."

An older married couple wanted to adopt Amanda. My birth parent's legal rights had been severed, so Amanda was available. The family was black and had two grown sons. They wanted a little girl, so Amanda moved immediately into their home.

A lot of people want to adopt babies and little kids. Amanda is loved, safe, and happy with her new family. I'm glad about that now.

"RJ is going to live in a foster home with an African American family," the agent said. "He'll be living near Amanda and her new home."

RJ's foster parents were a married couple with one biological child and three adopted kids. His foster home was just six houses away from where Mandy's new family lived. They got to see a lot of each other back then.

"What about me?" I asked, sniffling through my tears.

"I heard that you like animals, is that right?"

"Yes ma'am," I stopped crying. "I especially like dogs and cats."

"Well, you're going to live with a very nice lady who loves children and animals. I'm sure that you'll like living with her, Joshua."

The case worker drove me across town to meet LaTisha Owens and her family. Her house was sort of out in the country. She had two acres of land.

We drove into the driveway and the social worker cut the engine. Taking my hand she gave it a squeeze. She escorted me to the front door, which opened before we could knock or ring the bell.

"Well, you must be Joshua," LaTisha greeted me with a smile. "Come on in, Honey, and make yourself at home," she said, stepping aside and gesturing for us to enter.

LaTisha was a single black woman who already had seven kids living in her home. She had three biological babies from her marriage. After her divorce, she took in foster children. It wasn't unusual for her to adopt some of them.

The walls of her family room were covered with pictures of her big family. Some of those kids were grown-up by then with children of their own. LaTisha knelt down so that we were eye level with one another.

"My name is LaTisha Owens. My kids all call me 'Mom.' You can call me whatever feels right for you, OK?"

I nodded in understanding.

"Let me introduce you to the family, and we'll get you settled in."

LaTisha had adopted her oldest children when they were three, five, and six years old. Now they were teenagers. She pointed to each one and told me their names.

"Kids, this is Joshua," she introduced me to the crowd of friendly faces. "And this is Jabar, Lulu, and Adrianna."

"Hi Joshua."

"Nice to meet you."

"Welcome to the family, Joshua."

35

"This is Benjamin, my eight year old foster child," she said, resting her hands on his shoulders. "The two of you will be sharing a room."

"Hi," we spoke to one another.

"And this is Mitchell, who is five, Roberto, who just turned four and little Maria, who is only two years old. I've adopted them too."

Mitchell and Roberto waved at me. Maria ran to her mother and buried her face in LaTisha's neck.

I managed a weak "Hi," and quick wave of my hand.

The case worker excused herself and left.

"Joshua, I hear that you like animals, is that right?" LaTisha asked.

"Yes, ma'am," I answered quietly.

"We have quite a few around here. Would you like to see some of our animals now?"

"Sure, that would be great," I said, beginning to relax.

"Jabar, would you please get Britches and bring him to us? Joshua, would you mind sitting on the edge of this couch? When Britches arrives he'll want to meet you. He gets to know you by smelling you."

Jabar returned to the room carrying a fat, little, tan dog with a smashed in nose.

"This is Britches," Jabar announced. "He's a pug and very friendly. Don't worry, he won't bite you. First let him smell the back of your hand, and then you can pet him."

I extended my arm and his whiskers ticked my flesh. Reaching for his little velvet ears I started talking softly to him.

"I like the way you're petting Britches, Joshua," LaTisha said. "You have a gentle way with animals."

I grinned at her.

"Would you like to meet our Doberman? His name is Dakota. Some people are afraid of him because of his size, but he won't hurt you either," LaTisha assured me.

"Well, OK," I said cautiously. "If you promise that he isn't mean."

Jabar handed Britches to me and left the room once again. The pug curled up next to me and quickly fell asleep. Because he had a squished in nose, he began to snore. I thought that was hilarious. The rest of the family laughed along with me.

This time Jabar returned with a very large black and tan Doberman walking calmly by his side. Dakota didn't look like the Dobermans that I had seen before. His ears hung down. They hadn't been cropped to make them stand up and point towards the sky. His ears were left natural, and that made him look friendly. I liked Dakota right away.

"Dakota, sit," Jabar commanded, and the dog obeyed.

I extended my hand and he checked it out with his long nose.

"Is it OK to pet him now?"

"Yes," Jabar said.

I stroked his head and scratched behind his ears. Dakota stretched to lay his head in my lap. I took it as a good sign.

"He likes me," I said with pleasure.

"Indeed he does," LaTisha agreed.

"Would you like to meet my kitten?" Jabar asked.

I followed him to his room where I found a gray male tabby kitten named Tyler.

"You can play with him if you like," Jabar said. "He loves to chase this green feather that I got from our bird." He handed me the feather which had been tied to the end of a long blue string.

"Here kitty, chase the feather," I teased and dragged the feather along the ground. It wiggled and Tyler pounced on it and made me laugh.

"He's great, thanks for letting me play with him," I told Jabar.

"You're welcome, Joshua. Do you want to see the rest of our pets?"

I nodded and followed Jabar back to the family room where everyone had been waiting for us.

"Do you like snakes, Joshua?" LaTisha asked.

"Snakes?" I asked, not sure that I had heard her correctly.

"Yep, that's right," Lulu confirmed. "I have a corn snake."

She walked towards a large cage. It was sitting in the hallway on a table, at the other end of the room. The teenage girl opened the door and confidently lifted out the yellow and white reptile.

"This is Slim," Lulu said, draping him around her shoulders like a feather boa.

"Wow," I said laughing nervously as Lulu carried him back to where I was sitting.

"He's big," I said as Lulu held him by his tail with his head almost touching the ground. "He's as long as I am tall!"

Slim was yellow on top and white on the bottom. His quick tongue flicked in and out of his mouth. His black eyes stared at me.

"Want to hold him? It's OK, he isn't poisonous or anything."

I thought this was some kind of a test. I felt as though I had to hold the snake in order to prove myself to these kids.

"OK," I managed, mustering up my courage.

"Don't squeeze him, just relax," Lulu said as she placed the serpent in my open palms. The rest of the kids exchanged looks and nodded their approval.

I felt his long body move. It was like a wave of dominoes collapsing in sequence in my hands. It was amazing! I smiled, marveling at this amazing creature.

"It's time for his dinner; want to watch me feed him?"

Lulu took Slim from me and returned him to his cage. The rest of us followed. Opening a much smaller cage, Lulu lifted a live mouse by its tail, and dropped the rodent into Slim's private quarters. Lulu had bought the mouse at a pet store the day before. Slim needs to eat one live mouse every week.

Slim attacked the mouse with his mouth wide open. He swallowed it whole. His muscles contracted, as he pushed his dinner slowly down his body.

"Eeeeewwwww, gross!" I said. "Look, you can still see the shape of the mouse inside of him."

"That reminds me, it's time for our dinner too," LaTisha announced.

We all returned to the family room and everyone pitched in to make the evening meal.

# Chapter 6

## *Brothers and Sisters*

With such a big family and so many animals, we each had chores to do. One of mine was to feed the pig.

"Come on, Joshua, grab those food scraps and we'll go feed the pig," LaTisha told me after dinner that first night. She took me out to the barn to meet Stinkerboy.

She showed me how to feed him and get fresh water for his trough. Stinkerboy was a huge black pig. I swear he was the size of our bathtub! He didn't smell nice either, so I guess that's how he got his name. He had a long snout that wiggled a lot.

"Have you ever petted a pig, Joshua?" LaTisha asked. "The hair on his body is long and stiff. Want to feel?"

I reached over the rail and felt his wiry hair.

"That's weird," I agreed.

A horse nickered at the other end of the barn. She was greeting her owner and asking for her supper.

"Do you like horses?" LaTisha asked.

"I guess so, but I've never ridden one," I said.

"Come and meet Doll-girl. She's a twenty year old quarter horse."

"Oh," I said, "Does that mean that she's young or old?"

"Well, that's a good question. I guess by horse standards she's on the old side. But she still has plenty of get-up-and-go when she needs it."

Doll-girl came over to where we stood. She lifted her head over the rail and LaTisha began stroking her muzzle.

"May I pet her?"

"I think she'd like that," LaTisha said as she guided my hand gently down the mare's nose.

"I can feel her breath," I almost whispered, "It's warm. And her nose feels like velvet. Look at those long hairs on her nose."

"Her nose is called a muzzle, and you're right, it's very soft. I appreciate the way you behave around animals, Joshua. It's very calm and gentle."

"Thank you, ma'am." I beamed with pride.

Doll-girl is a bay mare. That means that her body is brown and her mane and tail are black."

"She's pretty, and I like the way she smells."

"I like that horsey smell, too," LaTisha agreed. "Let's get her some food and fresh water before it gets too dark, OK?"

We took care of our chores and returned to the house. The dishes and kitchen had been cleaned by the kids after dinner. Now they were all settled down together to watch the movie 'Stewart Little' on DVD.

"Joshua, why don't you go watch the movie with the other kids? I'll show you our bird later," LaTisha said. "You'll have the job of changing the newspaper in the bottom of his cage."

After the movie I went to LaTisha who was working on some papers.

"Excuse me, ma'am, may I please meet your bird now?"

"Certainly," she said smiling. "This is Jade, and he's a Quaker Parrot. He's smart and he talks."

Just then he greeted me, "Good-morning, good-morning, squawk, beautiful bird, beautiful bird."

I chuckled, "It's night time, silly bird! But he's right about being beautiful. What gorgeous feathers! I can see why Jabar used one of these feathers to make a toy for Tyler the cat."

I admired Jade's vibrant blue and green markings. He was strikingly handsome, but very messy. He'd throw his birdseed outside of the cage. It would get all over the kitchen floor, and it became my job to sweep it up.

"AHHHHHHHCCCChhhheeeewwwww!"

"God bless you!" LaTisha said smiling.

"Excuse me, ma'am, but the way Jade smells tickles my nose."

"I understand what you mean. A lot of people sneeze when they are around birds. Shall we put him to bed for the night?" LaTisha asked as she covered his cage with a sheet. "Nighty night," she told the bird.

"Sometimes Jade gets very loud," LaTisha said. "It's annoying. He'll start talking and then begin squawking. When he gets carried away, it's hard to get him quiet. That's when we put him in a 'time out.' You know what a time out is, don't you?"

"Yes, ma'am, a 'time-out' is when you sit quietly by yourself until you get your emotions under control. It gives you time to cool off and think about what you've done, and how you've been acting," I explained.

"Excellent, Joshua. I can tell that you and I are going to get along just fine," she said. "When Jade needs a 'time-out,' we cover him with the sheet like this, and tell him, 'Nighty, night.' Sometimes it's the only way to have a little peace and quiet in this house." LaTisha touched my shoulder.

I was starting to feel comfortable with my new foster mom. She was a pretty woman with big, brown, friendly eyes. She smiled and laughed a lot, and seemed happy.

LaTisha was nice to me and I liked living with her. After a couple of days, I was calling her "Mom." I secretly hoped that she would adopt me too, but she never did.

I got used to being part of a mixed race family. LaTisha and Adrianna were black. They wore their hair in corn rows and braids. Jabar was biracial, and his skin was a little lighter than mine. One of his parents was black, and one was white.

Lulu, Roberto and Maria were Hispanic. Roberto and Maria were biological brother and sister. They had the same birth parents and they looked alike.

Benjamin and Mitchell were each white. Benjamin was thin and had short, spiked red hair.

His face was covered with red freckles. The night before I moved to the Owens house, Ben had lost his two front teeth. Lucky for him, the tooth fairy had paid him a visit. Ben liked to jingle his four new shiny quarters in his pocket.

Mitchells' face looked a little odd. I could tell that something was different about him. LaTisha explained to me that Mitchell's birth mother drank a lot of alcohol when she was pregnant with him.

Mitch didn't talk very well. A lot of grown-ups couldn't understand what he was saying.

Mitchell was old enough to use the restroom, but he still had accidents. He still needed to wear a diaper. Mitchell laughed and smiled a lot. He was a fun kid, and we all got along with him.

When I stayed with the Owens' family, I practically lived in the same pair of comfortable old blue jeans. They were size 6 slim. I'd yank on my favorite blue t-shirt, pull up some mismatched socks, and grab my size 3 basketball shoes. I was built for speed, but dressed for comfort.

At first LaTisha kept my black nappy hair clipped short. After six months, I convinced her to let me grow an afro. I liked that it felt soft and puffy to my touch. Having an afro made me feel like the brothers I saw on TV. I wanted it to grow long enough for LaTisha to braid it for me.

I've always smiled a lot, and usually show my teeth.

"You have the most beautiful smile, Joshua," LaTisha would say. "Your pearly white ivories just light up the room."

LaTisha used to tell us, "Even though you kids don't look alike, you're all brothers and sisters in God's eyes."

# Chapter 7

## *A Miracle*

"LaTisha, I don't feel well." I complained one Sunday evening in early spring.

"What's the matter, honey?" She turned her attention to me.

"I keep coughing, I can't breathe, and my stomach hurts," I moaned and doubled over in pain.

"Lulu, get Joshua's coat for him. Jabar, you're in charge of the house. I'm taking him to Urgent Care."

She grabbed her purse and keys, and rushed me outside and into the van. I flopped across the back seat and closed my eyes. I must have quickly fallen asleep. Before I knew it, we were parked at the medical center and LaTisha was shaking me awake.

Slowly I crawled out of the car. I dragged myself to the front door of the Urgent Care Medical Clinic. Once inside, my legs gave out and I collapsed. Luckily, LaTisha caught me just before I hit the hard tile floor.

A male nurse scooped me up and carried me quickly into an exam room. He laid me on the table. Someone paged the doctor to hurry into the room.

"Dr. Bee, Dr. Bee, emergency in room #2; Dr Bee, emergency in room #2." The message filled the hallways. Medical staff and patients paid attention to the announcement. They were curious to know what was going on.

I was alert now, but having difficulty breathing. I was sucking air as if I had just run a 100 yard dash. My heart was racing. The nurse began taking my vital signs; my temperature, pulse, and blood pressure.

A pretty lady doctor entered room #2 and took charge of things. She was Dr. Bee, and she began asking LaTisha and me a lot of questions.

"What's your name, son? How old are you? Are you his mother? What are his symptoms? Where does it hurt? How long has he not felt well? Did he lose consciousness? How long was he out? Does he take any medication? Which ones and for what medical issues? Is he allergic to any medicines? Did he eat anything unusual last night or today?"

Dr. Bee fired questions at us, trying to figure out why I was so sick. She ordered x-rays of my chest. When she saw them, she realized that I was in big trouble.

"Joshua has serious problems with his lungs. He needs to be admitted to the hospital immediately. We'll send him by ambulance, and call ahead so they'll be expecting you," Dr. Bee said. "Good luck, Ms. Owens, be well, Joshua."

They wrapped me in a blanket and loaded me into a red ambulance. Even the wailing of the sirens didn't keep me from falling asleep on the way to the hospital emergency room.

When we arrived, I was immediately taken to the ICU, that's the Intensive Care Unit, for kids. I had just entered the building, and was already one of the sickest patients in the hospital.

Dr. Martin was my doctor in ICU. He was a young guy with a long brown pony tail and an easy smile. He ordered a bunch of tests on me that checked my blood and urine. He also took more x-rays. It was obvious to everyone that I was in very bad shape. I was rapidly getting worse.

Doc Martin said that I had something called Strep Pneumonia. The pneumonia made it hard for me to breathe. The doctor put me on a machine called a ventilator. It's like a respirator, and helped me get the oxygen I needed to stay alive.

While all of this was happening, my heart was still racing. It wasn't getting enough air, and I had a slight heart attack. That means that part of my heart muscle wasn't working. Thank God the respirator helped my heart get more oxygen, because I could have died!

Dr. Martin told LaTisha that I also had a very bad infection. It was called Septicemia. He started me on antibiotics to fight the infection.

"Ms. Owens, Josh is a very sick little boy. His kidneys are shutting down," the doctor explained to LaTisha.

"The kidneys clean the blood, and his have stopped working."

LaTisha was shaken by this news. She sat down on a chair in the ICU waiting room. Someone handed her a cup of water. She was stunned and stared into space for a moment.

My physician took a seat beside her. The bad news wasn't over yet. He leaned forward and very calmly gave her an update on my serious condition.

"Joshua has suffered a multiple system shutdown. His heart, lungs, and kidneys need assistance in order to work. His whole body is shutting down. We've given him drugs to put him into a medical coma. This is a very deep sleep. We hope that by doing this, his body can stay alive with the least amount of effort possible. He could die at any time," the doctor warned.

"We will continue to do all that we can for him, but it doesn't look good. I'm sorry. I recommend that you call your family together to say good-bye. You may want to start making funeral arrangements," Dr. Martin told my foster mom.

LaTisha sat paralyzed in her seat. She began to weep quietly. A nurse came to comfort her.

"Is there someone we can contact for you?" the nurse asked.

LaTisha jerked back to reality and sprang into action. "Joshua is my foster child. I need to call his caseworker. And I need to get in touch with his attorney."

During the next three days, my foster brothers and sisters came to the hospital to see me. They each wanted to say "good-bye." There was a lot of crying and sadness.

Someone found my birth father, Randall Radford Senior. They reached him by telephone and explained what was happening to me. My dad and Grandma Jodie came to the hospital to see me. By then, dad and my birth mother, DeShona, had separated. She had moved to some place in Tennessee.

Dad and Grandma Jodie shuffled quietly into my hospital room. My father staggered weakly to my bedside. He gently lifted my little hand and rested it in his own.

"You're my son, Joshua. In my heart you always have been, and always will be. I love you, baby boy. Please be strong and stay with us. We need you to live, son," My dad was crying as he pleaded with me. He prayed for me to survive.

"Jesus loves you, this I know, for the Bible tells me so. Little ones to Him belong. They are weak, but he is strong," Grandma quietly sang.

A hospital aide remembered that I was in foster care. The nurse realized that Dad's parental rights had been severed. My blood relatives were told they had to leave.

"I'm sorry, but the law no longer recognizes your connection to Joshua. You won't be allowed in his room. You aren't even supposed to have information on how he is doing. I'm sorry, but you'll have to leave now," the nurse sadly informed them. Dad and my grandmother kissed me and left my room.

That night my foster mom, caseworker, and court appointed lawyer were all sitting together in the waiting room. They had all come to the hospital to check on me.

"Josh needs to be on a kidney machine, and we don't have one here," Dr. Martin told the group. "We've located one at a different hospital. It's twenty miles away. Josh needs to be transferred immediately."

The grown-ups listened carefully. "Josh could die while he is being moved to another hospital. It's going to take a miracle to save him. But it's the only chance that he has to live."

They agreed that I should go to another hospital. LaTisha kissed me on the forehead. Together my foster mom, my caseworker, and my attorney watched as the medical team loaded me into the waiting ambulance. With flashing lights and blaring sirens, we sped into the darkness of the night.

I survived the transport to the new hospital. Within an hour I was hooked up to the kidney machine. Immediately it started working and cleaning my blood. I was still in a deep sleep, but my condition was improving.

I stayed in the ICU of this second hospital for a month. During that time I continued to have a tube down my throat to help me breathe. There were two other tubes in my body. They supplied food to my stomach.

I had needles in my arms giving me medicines and fluids. There were dozens of wires and tubes surrounding my body. I looked like fresh prey caught in the giant web of a spider.

During the week of my eighth birthday, the breathing tube was removed from my throat. LaTisha brought a chocolate sheet cake to the hospital to celebrate.

She shared it with all of the doctors, nurses, aids, and technicians who had been taking care of me. She thanked them for all that they had done, and were still doing to make me well again.

My foster sister, Adrianna, had come to visit. She was sitting by my bed, quietly reading to herself. There was a piece of cake sitting on a plate on the tray table in front of me. Adrianna decided she wanted the cake, so she reached for it.

"Don't even think about it," I threatened her with my hoarse voice.

"AAAAYYYY!" Adrianna jumped to her feet, throwing her book to the floor.

LaTisha ran into my room followed by several nurses. Adrianna stood across the room pointing to me on the bed.

"He's alive, he's awake. Josh just spoke to me!" she insisted. "Look at him!"

I was awakening. My eyes were half-opened. The nurses could tell that I was more alert than I had been earlier in the day. My medically induced coma had lasted for four long weeks. Now it was finally over.

A miracle had happened, and I had survived another near death experience. My recovery from this coma marks the 4$^{th}$ of my nine cat lives.

# Chapter 8

## *The Angel Kiss*

To prevent patients from getting bed sores, hospital workers usually move their patients around in the bed. Because everyone thought that I was going to die, nobody bothered to adjust me or the position of my head anymore.

As a result, I got a pressure sore. It came from lying in the same position for four weeks, while I was in a coma. The hair stopped growing at this spot on my head, and now it was bald.

My bald spot is oval like an egg. If you touch your thumb to your first finger, you can see the shape. That's about the size of it too.

"Hey baldie, what's on the back of your head?" Kids used to tease me. Even grown-ups asked me what happened. I was self-conscious about my bald spot. I got mad and embarrassed whenever anybody asked about it.

When I was in the fourth grade some guys at school were teasing me. I made up a wild story about how I got my bald spot.

"I'm from a tribe in Africa," I told them. "This mark is from my tribal initiation ceremony. Every male child from my tribe has a bald spot like mine. It means that we're accepted as men in our tribe. Are you a man yet?"

The guys believed me too! Ha! They left me alone and never teased me again.

When I met my adoptive mom, she kissed my bald spot and explained it this way.

"Well, Josh. That's your angel kiss. It's where the angel kissed you to awaken you; so that you could be my son, and I could be your forever Mom."

From then on we always called my bald spot, my angel kiss.

# Chapter 9

# Winterhaven

It was winter when I first met my forever mom. A forever mom can be different from your biological mother. A forever mom chooses you to be her child. She legally adopts you to make you her own. She loves and takes care of you. She's a mother that keeps you forever.

"It's almost Christmas and school is out for the winter break. What do you say we all go to Winterhaven some night this week?" LaTisha asked her family.

"What's Winterhaven?" I asked.

"That's a neighborhood in town where every house is decorated for the holidays," she said.

"The Winterhaven streets are filled with colored lights," Lulu said. "There are scenes of the first Christmas, with stables, Baby Jesus, Mary and Joseph. Some houses even have the Three Wise Men, shepherds and their sheep."

"Of course, there are plenty of Santa Clauses and reindeer on display too," Adrianna said. "Last year there was one house that had it all. It had the manger scene, Santa and his workshop, snowmen, and even giant candy canes."

"Hey, don't forget there was a railroad train that traveled all around the front yard," Jabar added.

"And they had blaring music and gave away free candy canes," said Adrianna. "It was great!"

"Winterhaven is a big deal every year. A lot of people visit it," LaTisha said. "And almost everyone brings a can or box of food to donate to the local food bank."

"What's a food bank?" I asked.

"The food bank gives food to people who need it. Nobody should ever have to go to bed hungry, especially kids!" she said rubbing my afro.

"There will be a lot of people and cars going to this event," LaTisha said. "So I have a plan. We'll park our van at a mall, and ride the free bus over to the entrance. We can walk the streets and enjoy the sights, then get back on the bus and return to our van. This way, we can avoid all of that traffic," LaTisha said, pleased with herself.

On the evening of our outing, the sky was filled with dark gray clouds. The temperature was dropping, and we could smell the possibility of snow in the air. The sky turned into night as we waited at the mall for the bus. We were bored just standing around waiting.

"Got-cha, you're it!" Lulu yelled. She brushed Adrianna on the back with her hand, and took off running in the opposite direction.

Some of the kids were playing tag. The game was fun and might even help them get warm. We were all anxious to get on the bus and out of the harsh wind.

I had forgotten my hat and gloves and was already cold. Instead of playing tag, I knelt down to conserve my heat. I pulled up my jacket collar, tucked my chin against my chest, and shoved my hands into the pockets of my coat.

LaTisha was chatting with a couple of white women that I didn't know. Apparently, she had talked with one of them on the phone about adoption. That lady had told LaTisha that she wanted to adopt a little boy.

LaTisha invited her to join us at Winterhaven. That way she and LaTisha could talk in person, and the potential adoptive mom could meet LaTisha's kids.

I had overheard LaTisha's conversation on the phone just three days earlier. I heard my foster mom say, "One of my foster boys needs a forever home. He's eight years old and available for adoption. He is very sweet, and his name is Joshua," I heard her say.

"Kids, come over here please," LaTisha said.

We gathered around her, and she introduced each of us by name. Finally, she pointed to me and said, "and this is Joshua."

Poking my head from inside of my collar I gave a little nod. I looked briefly at the women, but didn't smile. Like a turtle, I ducked my head back into my cover. I was trying to be cool.

"These women are friends of mine," said LaTisha. "This is Jamie and this is her sister Julie."

"Hi," my brothers and sisters said in unison. "Nice to meet you."

I kept my head down and remained silent.

"Bus!" Jabar yelled, and we all scrambled to get on and take our seats.

"You sit with me, Joshua," LaTisha said. She positioned herself next to the window, and wrapped her arm around me. I buried myself in her cloak, and snuggled up against her to get warm.

The sisters we had just met were sitting across from LaTisha and me. Feeling shy, yet curious, I peeked at them every now and then. Each time I looked, one of them was watching and smiling at me.

It was a short ride to Winterhaven. The bus turned onto a brightly illuminated residential street. The brakes moaned and the bus sighed, as we eased to a stop.

"Watch your step folks, and enjoy your visit," our bus driver said. He was a thin black man with a shaved head and a thin moustache. "Buses depart from this location every half hour, to take you back to the mall." He winked and handed me a grape Tootsie Pop, as I passed his seat. "Have fun, son."

The trees were draped with strands of glimmering lights. Red, yellow, blue, and green globes hung like precious stones from a necklace. Even the rooftops and windows of the houses glowed with thousands of twinkling sparks. It reminded me of sparklers on the Fourth of July; each one being lighted by a match at the same time.

"Come on, children," LaTisha said, "Let's hustle off this bus and get moving."

Shivering with excitement, I hopped down from the bus onto the frozen earth.

"I've never seen so many Christmas lights in one place before. Let's go!" I pleaded, grabbing her hand and pulling her into the street.

We followed the crowd into the festive night air. Jabar, Lulu, and Adrianna led the way. They joined arms and sang Christmas carols. Jabar is a very good singer. It was comforting to hear his strong voice carry the melodies and messages of each song.

"Turn right at this corner, kids," LaTisha said.

We strolled up one street and down another. By the end of the night, I was worn out from our hours of hiking. We probably wore down five miles worth of shoe tread during our walk that evening.

"Should we take this bus, Mom?" Lulu asked.

"Yes, if everyone is here."

My foster mom did a nose count. When she was satisfied that her brood was intact, she stepped up into the vehicle and found a seat.

Following her lead, I pulled myself onto the bus and dropped down next to her.

Wondering who else was riding with us, I leaned forward to scope out the rows of faces. Immediately, I spotted the sisters that we had met earlier. One of them spotted me too, so I jumped back in my seat and pretended to hide.

Slowly inching forward, I peeked again. Busted! She caught me looking. I giggled and pressed my back against the seat. For the rest of the ride we played a silly game of hide-and-peek.

"This is where we get off," LaTisha announced to the family.

She and I climbed down from the bus. I turned to her, tugged on her coat sleeve and said, "I want to give that lady a hug."

She looked puzzled. "What lady, Joshua?"

"Your friend, that white lady in the purple jacket."

The sisters stepped off the bus. The one who played the pecking game with me wore a purple coat. I looked up at her and lifted my arms in the air.

This was my invitation for her to pick me up. She gave me a small welcoming smile, and lifted me into her arms. She held me for a long time. Her grip felt safe and confident. Her soft cheek warmed my frozen face. I turned my nose to her skin and breathed in her smell. It was foreign, yet pleasant to my nostrils. Then she stood me back on the ground.

"I guess I'd better introduce myself again, Joshua," she said. "My name is Jamie and this is my sister, Julie." She motioned towards her sister who was standing nearby. I could tell that they were sisters, they looked almost like twins.

"Hi," I greeted them, flashing my pearly whites.

I shivered from exposure to the cold temperatures. My fingers felt like they had turned into icicles. Jamie took both of my hands in hers.

"My goodness, Joshua, your little hands are frozen," she said.

As she blew warm air on them, my hands began to thaw. I liked that she was caring for me and giving me special attention.

"Shall we walk with you to your car?" Jamie asked.

The sisters escorted us to the van. All of the time, Jamie held both of my hands in hers. When we reached the car, she lifted me up for another embrace.

Jamie put me down, "See ya later alligator. Good night, LaTisha, 'bye kids. Thanks for inviting us to come along tonight."

"See ya!" I shouted climbing into the van and taking my seat.

LaTisha honked her horn and drove quickly away. Looking out of the back window, I saw that Jamie was still watching me.

I waved and she waved back; we each smiled. I felt a shock of electricity flash through my body. It reached all the way down to my toes. I was happy, and for the first time that night, I felt warm all over.

# Chapter 10

## *Two New Friends*

"Are you hungry?" LaTisha asked me as we entered the golden arches of McDonalds.

"Yes, ma'am!" I said with a grin.

I skipped to keep up with her long strides. We were having one of our special one-on-one outings. Every week, LaTisha made a date to spend time alone with one of her kids. Today was my turn for her undivided attention.

"What would you like?" she asked.

"A kid's meal," I answered.

"Excuse me? I don't think I heard you correctly."

"May I have a kid's meal, please?" I rephrased my words, this time remembering my manners.

"That's much better, Joshua, I heard you clearly that time."

"What's the prize anyway?" I was anxious to know what toy I would be getting.

"It's a glow-in-the-dark ball. I don't think you have one."

LaTisha placed my order with the clerk, and ordered her favorite. She loved her salad with mandarin oranges and strong black coffee. Within minutes we were seated in a booth.

"Mummmmmmm, this is great!" I announced. "Thank you for lunch, Mom, and for spending time with me."

"It's such a pleasure dining with a young man who remembers his manners," LaTisha said proudly.

I grinned delivering a salty potato stick into my mouth. LaTisha was quiet; she always paused in prayer before eating her meal.

For a few minutes we sat quietly together, focused on our food.

"Hey, LaTisha, Hi Joshua!" came a greeting from someone entering the restaurant.

We looked at the door, and saw Jamie, the woman we had met at Winterhaven last week. Jamie smiled, waved, and came over to our table.

She had someone with her and began the introductions.

"LaTisha, Joshua, I'd like you to meet my partner, Brooke. Brooke, these are the folks I was telling you about. This is Joshua, and his foster mom, LaTisha Owens. I met them last week at Winterhaven."

Brooke shook hands with LaTisha and me. "It's nice to meet you both. I heard you had a great time the other night," Brooke said. "I'm sorry I missed it."

We talked a while about Winterhaven. Then Jamie and Brooke excused themselves to get in line to order something to eat.

"Would you like them to join us?" LaTisha asked me.

"Sure!" I said with a smile.

The grown-ups talked while we ate. We learned that Brooke is a veterinarian. That means that she is a doctor for animals. Brooke and Jamie own an animal hospital and work together. It's called the Family Cat and Dog Clinic.

"May I please be excused?" I asked my foster mom. "I've finished my burger."

She nodded 'OK' and I ran to the play area. The room was filled with bright yellow, green, and red tunnels. To me it was a giant octopus. I was anxious to explore inside of its body and climb throughout the legs.

Six ladders gave me access to this monstrous creature. Four small round windows became his eyes. I threw off my shoes and climbed into the beast.

"Hey, everybody, look up here!" I called to the adults as I peered out one of his eyes.

I stuck my head through a portal and waved. They spotted me, smiled, and waved back. Dropping to my hands and knees, I pulled myself higher into one of the tubes. I was headed for this guy's guts.

At each window I poked my head out to see if anyone was watching.

Brooke and Jamie always were and we waved. Then I'd disappear again, only to find my way to another body part and a different window.

I came to a slide that landed in a tub filled with squishy 'Nerf' balls.

"Ahhhhhhhhhhhhhhhhhh
Ahhhhhhhhhhhhhhhhhhh
Ahhhhhhhhhhhhhhhhhhh," I filled my lungs and exhaled hard as I belted out my loudest Tarzan call ever.

"Joshua," scolded LaTisha, "not so loud!" LaTisha giggled and shook her head. "He's got a great imagination, that boy," LaTisha told our guests.

I jumped onto the slide and landed in the tub of balls. Swooshhhhhhh.

I was almost buried under the soft round spheres.
"GGGGRRRROOOOWWWWLLLL!
SSSSNNNNAAAARRRRLLLL!"

I became the monster exploding from under the blanket of balls. I tossed them into the air in all directions. I laughed with delight.

"OK," announced LaTisha, "it's time to go, Josh. Please find your shoes and put them back on your feet."

After a bit of searching, I found mine in the pile of cast off shoes. I stuck my favorite sneakers on my feet. I had them on the wrong feet but didn't care. I stuffed the laces down into the sides.

"It was nice seeing you again," LaTisha said to Jamie, "and a pleasure meeting you, Brooke."

"Thank you, I really enjoyed meeting each of you," Brooke answered.

LaTisha took my hand and we said goodbye. We began walking toward the parking lot.

"Wait a sec," I begged.

I ran back to give Jamie and Brooke each a hug.

"See ya later, alligator!" I said.

"After while crocodile," Jamie and Brooke smiled and said together.

I ran to catch up with LaTisha and reached for her hand. We walked to the van.

"It looks like you've made some new friends, Joshua," LaTisha said.

"Yeah, now I have two new friends," I announced with pride.

# Chapter 11

## *Quality Time*

Rrriiinnnggg, Rrriiinnnggg…

"Hello? Just a minute please. Joshua, telephone," Adrianna called out to me the next evening. I stopped playing tag with Benjamin and Mitchell, and ran to her. She handed the phone to me.

"Hello?" I spoke timidly. I never got any phone calls and wondered who was on the line.

"Hi Josh," came a familiar voice. "It's Jamie, how are you?"

"Good."

"I'm glad to hear that. Hey, Honey, I was wondering if you wanted to go to a movie with me this weekend?"

I asked LaTisha if it was OK. She thought it was a great idea. We had a good time, so Jamie, Brooke and I started doing things together every week.

"Mom, can we go to Mt. Lemmon and play in the snow today?" Jabar asked LaTisha on Sunday morning. "It's been snowing and the TV weatherman says there's at least a foot of snow on the summit."

LaTisha thought it was a grand idea. She invited Jamie and Brooke to go along. Brooke was busy, so Jamie went with me.

"Mom, is it OK if I ride with Jamie?" I asked. It was fine with her, so Jamie picked me up at my foster home. We headed up the mountain road with me belted into the back seat.

I'd never been up the mountain before, so this was a new and exciting experience for me. The road curved back and forth like a snake. Each turn took us closer to the top.

"Duck your head," Jamie said. "We're headed for a tunnel." We dropped our heads and I didn't lift mine until we exited the other side of the small tube. "Wow!" I said lifting my head, "it looks just like Heaven!"

Everywhere I looked there were tall evergreen trees. Their branches were heavy with fresh white powder.

"This is a scene from a Christmas card," I told Jamie.

"Hey look. There's my mom's van."

We spotted LaTisha's van parked in the lot up ahead. We pulled off the road and parked beside her.

My foster brothers and sisters were already having fun. The teenagers carried their sleds up the hill, while the little kids made snow angels.

"Have you ever made a snow angel, Josh?" Jamie asked.

"I've never even seen snow until today."

"Let's get you started then. I think you'll make excellent snow angels." Jamie lay down on the bed of white down, and showed me how to move my arms and legs. I followed her lead, and was proud of my first snow angel.

Jabar threw a snowball, hitting Adrianna in the leg. "Oops, are you all right? I'm sorry if I hurt you."

"You're dead meat, Jabar!" she said laughing, and fired a snowball back at him.

Within minutes things had erupted into a full scale battle. Luckily, the snow was dry and powdery. Most of the balls fell apart before they found their marks. We fell into the snow drifts laughing. It was a blast.

"I'll race you down the hill," said Jabar to anyone who would listen.

Always up for a challenge, Adrianna and Lulu each grabbed a sled and started down the mountain.

"Last one down is a rotten egg!" Adrianna shouted.

I watched as they bounced over the moguls and landed in the snow. Anxious to give it another try, they hurried back up the hill.

"Come on, Josh," said Jabar. "Jump on."

I sat down in front of him and away we flew. The snow hit me in the face, stinging my cheeks. I closed my eyes and trusted Jabar's steering. I was grateful when we slowed to a stop.

"How about I ride behind you next time?" I said.

Jabar nodded in agreement. We trudged our way back to the top of the run. Three more times down the hill and I had enough of the cold.

71

"Jamie, I'm fffrrreeeezzzziiiinnnngggg," I said through chattering teeth.

"Let's get you warmed up, then. We're heading for the car," she said to LaTisha.

Jamie turned on the motor of her red Toyota. "Hurry up, little engine," she said. "We need to get some heat in this cab to warm Josh. Honey, take off your wet boots and drop them in the back, on the floor. Climb over the consol and get into this blanket," she said, laying a kid-sized, blue 'Smokey the Bear' sleeping bag in the empty seat. "It has a zipper there on the side."

Eagerly, I kicked off my wet shoes and climbed into the front seat. It felt great snuggling into the comforter.

"Do you like hot chocolate? I made this for you."

Jamie handed me a cup. The warm cup felt good in my hands. The beverage was hot and sweet and warmed me from the inside out.

"Would you like me to read to you while we wait for the others?" She asked.

"That would be great," I said. Jamie adjusted her seat to make room for me on her lap.

She read the story *Balto, The Sled Dog.* She finished the book just as everyone else arrived at LaTisha's van to go home. I was glad to get off the mountain and back into some dry, warm clothes. I hate being cold!

"I thought maybe you'd like to go with me to visit my parents tonight, Josh." Jamie told me after I had changed. "My mom makes the best hamburger in the state, and my folks are looking forward to meeting you. What do you say?"

We went to see her parents. Compared to me, they were old, maybe even ancient. Jamie's mother made me a hamburger with ketchup only. That's the way I like them. Mine was perfect.

"Would you like a bowl of Cookies-n-Cream ice cream, Josh?" Jamie's dad asked me after dinner.

"Oh, yes, please! Cookies-n-Cream is my favorite!"

72

Before the night was over, he dipped me two bowls of the sweet treat. I was in seventh heaven. Before we left their house, Jamie's dad showed me how to juggle with three tennis balls. I had fun visiting them.

I began spending even more time with Jamie and Brooke. We saw each other during the week instead of just on weekends now.

"Do you like basketball, Josh?" Brooke asked. "We have tickets to the U of A women's game. Would you like to go?"

"Sure!" I said with a smile. "As long as LaTisha says that it's OK."

We went to a game and I was impressed by the players. They were really good. Jamie says that I'm a good player, too. I like dribbling and scoring three pointers the best.

"This team is called the Wildcats," Jamie said. "Look over there, do you see her? That's Wilma Wildcat," she said pointing to the sideline.

A human sized wildcat was walking upright along the basketball court. Wilma paraded all around the court and went up into the stands.

"The college team's colors are red and blue," Brooke told me. "That's why Wilma wears a little red skirt with a blue top, like the cheerleaders."

"She has a red bow that she wears over her ear," Jamie said. "It matches her red and blue polka-dotted shoe laces."

Wilma had a big head and a very short tail. She didn't talk, but I understood what she wanted when she came over to our seats. She motioned for me to join her in the aisle.

I climbed over Jamie and Brooke to the stairway. Wilma put her arm around me and Brooke took our photo.

I slapped her paw for a high five. I laughed and went back to my seat. From that day on, Wilma came to see me at each home game. We'd meet in the stairs, give each other a hug, and high five, and finally bump fists.

Half-time was my favorite part of every game. That's when kids from the crowd got invited to play games on the basketball floor. One time, I was asked to participate.

"Heck, yes!" I said.

It was hard for me to sit still during the first half. I was anxious to get onto the court. With three minutes left in the first half Jamie turned to me.

"OK, head on down, have fun and good luck." I gave Jamie and Brooke a high five, and scooted out of my seat.

When the buzzer sounded, ten tired college players exited the floor heading for their locker rooms. At the same time, ten energetic kids immediately replaced them at center court. The college students set-up nine folding chairs.

"We're going to play a basketball version of musical chairs," one guy with long sideburns and a shaggy beard said. "Each kid will have a basketball. When the music starts you need to split up. Half of you go to that basket," he said pointing to one end of the court. "And the rest of you dribble towards the other end." He swung around and indicated the opposite side of the floor.

"You need to score a basket, and then get back to the chairs as fast as you can. When the music stops, grab a chair and sit down. After each round, a player and a chair will be taken away. Does everybody understand?"

Ten heads went up and down with anxious nods. It was time for him to stop talking and let us do our thing.

I was on that night. My ball handling was controlled, and my shots were hitting. I was one of three kids still playing after several rounds.

There were two of us guys and one girl left. The other guy was about a head taller than I was. I'd guess that he was maybe ten. The girl was about my size and age. She was really good, too! Remember now, I was only eight years old when this happened.

The music started and we were off. I raced down the court and shot a three pointer. It swished through the net. I was the first kid back to the chairs.

"Whooo-hooo!" Jamie and Brooke cheered from the stands. "Way to go, Joshie!"

The other boy missed his shot twice, and the girl beat him back to the seats. Now there were only two of us left and we were down to only one chair.

The crowd was on their feet, cheering and clapping. My heart pounded inside of my chest. The song played again and I took off in a fast break towards my hoop.

I tried a bank shot, no good. I grabbed the rebound and hit a lay-up. I sprinted back to the chair. The girl and I bumped our hips together as we each tried to sit at the same time. It was a tie!

I was pumped! I took a deep breath and tried to settle myself before we started our tie-breaker. At the very first note, I was on my feet. My shoes were pounding against the floor as quickly as I could move.

My first shot missed, and so did my second. Lucky for me, my opponent was also having difficulty finding the hole. I snatched my rebound and tried a left handed lay-up. It dropped through the net. I sprinted towards center court. I arrived just after she took possession of the folding metal seat. Game over.

"Congratulations, that was great!" I smiled at her as we shook hands.

"You're really good," she said. I liked the compliment.

"Thanks, you too."

We panted to catch our breath as we walked off the court together. The crowd gave us a standing ovation. It felt as though each of us had won.

"Nice job, young man, congratulations, there, fella." Strangers told me what a great sport I was. They patted me on the back. Men, women, and children gave me high fives. It was tight!

I made my way back to Jamie and Brooke.

"You were awesome, Josh!" they said hugging me tightly. "We're so proud of you," Brooke told me slapping my hand with a high five, a low five, and a fist punch.

"I'm so impressed with your sportsmanship," Jamie said. "That was outstanding." She shook my hand then punched fists with me too.

The people sitting around us were grinning from ear to ear. I felt like a hero, and I loved it!

# Chapter 12

## *The Question*

I didn't pay much attention to what happened during the second half of the game. I guess I was too pumped up from my half-time activities.

After the final buzzer sounded, I took hold of Jamie's and Brooke's hands and led them to the car. Brooke drove the Toyota and Jamie sat in the back seat with me.

"Joshua, do you know what it means to be adopted?" Jamie asked me as she held my hand in hers.

"Sure," I answered, "It means that you keep someone forever and ever."

"That's right, Honey. Well, I'd like to adopt you and be your forever mom," said Jamie. "I want you to be my son. What do you think of that idea?"

"I love it," I said cheering. I reached out and gave Jamie a hug.

"Now can I call you Mom?"

"That works for me, Son."

"Beeeeeeeeep, Beeeeeeeeeeep, Beeeeeeeeeeeep, Beeeeeeeeeeep!"

Brooke celebrated on the car horn. She flashed the caution lights too. We were celebrating!

"Honey, look at our hands," Mom said to me.

"I know, black, white, racial," I looked at the back of my small black hand resting on top of her white palm.

"Some people may not like that you have a white mother. Some folks might be mean to you."

"It doesn't bother me," I said, "We'll deal with it."

"Honey, do you know what it means if someone is gay?"

"I think so. It means that boys like boys and girls like girls."

"That's right. And a gay couple means that two men, or two women understand, love, and support one another. They relate better to each other than to someone of the opposite sex. They are partners and are happiest when they are together. Does that make sense?"

I nodded that I understood. Brooke stopped the car at a red light and turned around to look at us in the back seat.

"If I adopt you, then you'll have two moms, Brooke and me, because we're a couple. How do you feel about that?"

"I love you and Brooke, so if you're a couple, it's fine with me. Having two moms would be great. What should I call you, Brooke?"

"What feels right to you?" Brooke asked.

"How about Mama B?" I said.

"That's perfect," she said taking my hand. I squeezed her hand quickly before the light turned green and she drove off.

"So when are you going to 'dopt me?"

"Well, it takes a while to get all of the paperwork done. In Arizona it isn't legal for an unmarried couple to adopt a child. And two men or two women can't legally marry in this state, so we can't adopt you together," Mom said.

"That's stupid! I want both of you to be my moms."

"We agree with you, Honey, and we don't understand that way of thinking," Brooke said. "We love you and want to be your parents."

"What do you have to do?"

"I'll be your legal parent," Mom said, "and Brooke will be your second mom."

"How do we do that?"

"I need to attend classes about adopting an older child," Mom said, "because that's what you are. A lot of people only want to adopt babies. I know that you've had some rough times, and I need to learn what to expect, and how to help you. Does that make sense?"

"I guess so," I admitted. "I'm just glad that you're going to 'dopt me."

"You know, Honey, there are so many kids, of all ages, who need loving homes. And I'll tell you this; to me you are the pick of the litter."

"What does that mean?" I asked.

"The pick of the litter means that, of all the kids in the world who need a mom, you're the best. And you're the one that I choose for me."

"Wow, I'm the pick of the litter. So when you finish your classes, will I be your son then?"

"I need to do more than just attend classes. Some social workers will come out to my house."

"Why?"

"Because they need to see if my home is a safe place for you to live. And they'll ask me a lot of questions."

"How come?"

"It's their job to make sure that I'd be a good mother for you."

"Heck, all they have to do is ask me. I'll tell them that you'll be the greatest mom!" I said.

"Thanks for the support, Honey," Jamie said smiling.

"Some people who know me really well will write letters for me. They'll explain why they think I would be a good mother. The state will run a background check on me."

"What's a background check?"

"They look into my life. It's their job to make sure I'm a good person, and not a criminal or someone who would hurt you. The state is very careful about making sure children are adopted into good loving homes."

"That's a lot of stuff to get done."

"Yes, it is, but you're worth it," Jamie said.

Six months later, Jamie's application to adopt was accepted. I finally got to move in with her. I liked calling her "Mom" and we started making up our own routines.

Whenever we wanted to hug, I'd jump up into her arms for what we called a "jump hug." We'd squeeze each other tight. It was one of our favorite things to do. I knew that I was going to love being 'dopted.

# Chapter 13

## *The Pool Party*

"Hi Jamie, we're having a pool party next Sunday afternoon," LaTisha told Mom over the phone, "We'd love for you all to join us."

"That sounds great, what shall we bring?" Mom asked.

"How about dessert?"

"You got it, see you then."

The party started at 3:00 p.m. As soon as we got to LaTisha's house, I ran to the bathroom to change into my swimming trunks.

"Joshie, please be careful and stay in the shallow end," Mom said. "We need to be able to see you at all times."

Most of my former foster brothers and sisters were already in the pool. I quickly jumped into the shallow end.

Splash!

"Hi, guys!" I called to them.

"Hey, Josh, good to see you," Lulu said in response. There were a lot of adults sitting around the pool supervising their kids in the water. Mom and Brooke were standing at the end of the pool. They were watching me, and talking with Jabar, who was wearing his street clothes.

"Where's Josh?" Brooke asked. "I just saw him a few seconds ago. I keep looking for his angel kiss, but I now I can't find it."

Brooke had been looking for my angel kiss on the back of my head. It's my special identification. She got worried when she couldn't find it.

"There he is," Jabar said pointing to me on the bottom of the deep end of the pool.

"Jabar, get ready to go in," Mom said.

Jabar jumped in the water. Mom and Brooke came around to the side of the pool. Brooke was already dialing 911 on her cell phone, calling an ambulance for help.

Jabar pulled me up from the bottom of the pool, and laid me across my mom's lap. I was very limp. My eyes were big, white, and rolled back into my head. I was unconscious and not breathing.

"Joshie, NO!" Mom yelled trying to stop what was happening. She stared at me in disbelief. Mom froze in confusion and shock. She couldn't think of what she should do next.

A lady that Mom just met ran up to her. She suspected that I wasn't breathing, and that my heart wasn't beating either.

"Who knows CPR?" she asked.

"I do!" Mom realized, snapping the spell and taking action. "I'll breathe, you do the chest compressions."

They started doing CPR on me.

The lady was pushing on my chest to make my heart beat, and my mom was blowing air into my lungs.

After a few seconds, I started to throw up some water. Mom turned my head to the side, so that I wouldn't choke. Brooke felt for my pulse.

"His heart is beating, stop compressions," Brooke said.

The lady stopped pushing on my chest. I was breathing on my own and opened my eyes.

Mom looked at LaTisha's daughter, Adrianna.

"Adrianna, please get my purse from out of our car, it's not locked. My purse is on the floor of the front passenger side, bring it to me."

She turned her attention to Lulu.

"Lulu, Josh's dry clothes are on the hamper of the guest bathroom. They are a pair of green sweat pants and a shirt. Please get them for me now."

Adrianna and Lulu did as they were asked. Mom dried me with a towel, and put dry clothes on my shivering body.

By then, emergency medical technicians, or EMTs arrived at the pool. They took over caring for me. They covered me with a blanket and put me in the back of an ambulance.

"Are you his mom?" one EMT asked. "Why don't you jump in the cab with me?"

"I'll follow in our car," Mama B said. "Which hospital?"

"St. John's is the closest, we'll go there."

Mom rode in the cab with the driver. We quickly traveled to the emergency room, or ER, of St. John's Hospital. Mama B arrived as we pulled up to the door. The EMTs pulled me from the ambulance and wheeled me into the exam room.

"How long was he under water? Did someone perform CPR? How long did you do that?" The ER doctors began firing questions at my parents. They were trying to determine how much damage had been done to my brain. The longer I was without oxygen, the worse my chances for making a full recovery.

"It's hard to say, I'd guess he was under water for only a few seconds," Mama B said. "We did CPR for about 20 seconds before he regained consciousness."

"Let's get some x-rays and test his blood," the ER doctor ordered. The x-ray films showed a lot of gas caused from the CPR.

"Because of the coma he experienced a few months ago, I'd like Joshua to stay in the hospital tonight for observation," the doctor said. "We'll put a cot into his room for you, Ms. Carson."

"Thank you. I'd appreciate that," Mom said.

Mama B left the hospital, and Mom stayed overnight with me. Mama B came to the hospital the next morning.

"Hi, Joshie, how are you, Sweetheart?" she asked, kissing each of us on the cheek.

"How are you doing, Honey?" she asked my mom.

"I didn't sleep very well," Mom said. "Every time I closed my eyes, I had flashbacks of the near drowning. I'd see Jabar handing Josh's limp body to me, and laying him across my lap."

"Oh, that's terrible, I'm so sorry," Mama B said. "What's the word from the doctors?"

"They've ordered more tests. They want to be sure that he's all right," Mom said.

The doctor came to see me. "Josh is improving, but just as a precaution, I'd like him to spend a second night in the hospital."

Mom stayed in the hospital with me the second night too.

A short Hispanic woman walked into my room. "I thought Josh might be getting a little bored," the nurse said as she handed a Nintendo game to me.

"Thank you, ma'am!" I said, my eyes getting big with anticipation.

My folks sat at the edge of my bed and watched me play.

"Joshie, what happened to you in the pool?" Mom asked me.

"Well, I was in the deep end, holding onto the side of the pool with my hands. I did that a lot when I lived with LaTisha. My hands slipped, and I started going down under the water," I said.

"But, Honey," Mom asked, "why didn't you kick and splash and call for help?"

"I did call for help," I defended myself. "I yelled 'MOM!' But you couldn't hear me, 'cause I was under water."

"Oh, Sweetheart," Mom hugged and kissed me. Mama B gave my hand a squeeze, and kissed my forehead. They had tears in their eyes.

"Do you remember anything from when you were under the water, Honey?" Mama B asked.

"Well, I remember that it was very quiet and peaceful," I said softly. "May I go back to playing my game now, please?"

I picked up the game controls and focused on the action on the screen.

"You two will probably think this is weird," Mom said to us, "but I had a premonition about this accident."

"What's a prem-a, prem-a...?" I asked her.

"Premonition," Mom said, helping me with the word. "That's when you sort of know that something is going to happen before it does. On the drive over to LaTisha's house that day, I had a feeling there was going to be a near drowning. I wondered how serious an accident would have to be, to justify calling 911," she said.

"Really?" Mama B asked, looking astonished.

"Yes, somehow I knew that Josh would be involved. I thought I might need his insurance information. So when I got out of the car, I intentionally put my purse in a spot where anyone could easily find it."

"That's amazing," Mama B said.

"I even watched to see where Josh put his sweat clothes after he changed into his swim trunks. I knew that they were on the hamper in the guest bathroom. I felt like he might need them in a hurry."

"When we were talking with Jabar, something kept drawing my attention to the bottom of the pool. If I ignored it, the feeling persisted. There was a black spot there, but I thought it was a marking on the pool floor."

"I wore my black swim trunks that day," I said. "They were the trunks that I begged you to let me buy."

Mom pulled me to her. She held me close and continued with her story.

"If I looked away from that spot, my attention was immediately drawn back to it," Mom told us. "I believe one of two things happened. One is that Josh and I have an extremely strong bond to each other. Somehow, in my mind, I heard him calling me. I knew he needed help even though he was under water."

"That makes sense." Mama B agreed.

"The second explanation is that your guardian angel saved you, Josh. Your angel tried to warn me of the accident on the way to the party. Then she kept trying to get my attention when you were in trouble in the water."

"Don't forget that Jabar is also your hero, Josh. He jumped into the water and pulled you out before you drowned," my other mom said.

"Joshie, please don't ever scare us like that again," Mom said to me. "We were so afraid that we'd lost you."

"I'm sorry," I answered softly. "I didn't mean to scare you."

"Joshie, Honey, when you were born nine years ago, you didn't come from my body. But two days ago I breathed my air into your lungs," Mom looked me straight in the eyes. "There's no question that you are my son."

Mom was crying as we rocked together in silence for a few seconds. Mom kissed my cheeks, nose, and my forehead. Then she kissed my bald spot.

"Thank you, God and Guardian Angel. Thank you Jabar and Brooke and CPR lady. Thank you EMTs and all of the doctors and nurses. Thank you beautiful angel kiss," she whispered.

Not everybody recovers from a near downing. I'm very grateful that I have the luck of a cat. And that's the story of my cat life #5.

# Chapter 14

## *Facing My Fears*

The day after I got out of the hospital, I had a swimming lesson at the YMCA.  I had been taking lessons before I nearly drowned.

"Maybe we should get you a life jacket to wear in the pool," Mom said.

My folks were worried that I would be afraid of the water.

"No way!  I'm not afraid of the water," I said.

We went to my swimming lessons and told the teacher about what happened.

"Josh, I'd like you to sit at the edge of the pool today, and dangle your feet in the water," the teacher instructed me, so that's what I did.

Later that same week, I had another swimming lesson.   By that time, Mom had bought me some bright yellow swim trunks.  No more black trunks for me.  During this class I got in the water and participated with the other kids.

Three weeks later, on the last day of swimming classes, everyone was supposed to go down the slide.  Here the water was over our heads, but only by a couple of inches.  As a final test, we were to jump off of the diving board.  The board was at the deep end of the pool.

My folks were watching me as I stood at the bottom of the slide.  I took a deep breath, and slowly climbed to the top.  Sitting down, I held onto the sides.  Slowly, I eased my way go down the slope and dropped into the cool liquid.

My teacher was waiting for me in the water in case I needed help.  I was fine and swam to the edge of the pool.  I was proud of myself, and had gained back some of the confidence that I had lost.

Then it was time for the diving board.  I was afraid of going under water in the deep end of the pool.  I was afraid of drowning.  I was in no hurry to get in the water.  I stood at the end of the line.  Finally, it was my turn.  I stepped onto the 12' plank.

I pretended to blow out 100 candles on a birthday cake, by taking a deep breath and blowing out hard. This gave me fresh oxygen in my lungs. I took another big breath and held it. Slowly allowing the air to escape from my lips, I walked to the edge of the board.

My teacher was treading water in the deep end. She was there in case I panicked and got into trouble.

"You can do this, Josh," she said to me. "I'm here if you need me, but you won't."

I didn't bounce, but simply stepped off the end and plunged into the pool. I bobbed once and quickly came to the surface. Grinning from ear to ear I yelled, "Yeah!"

My teacher turned me towards the pool ladder, and I eagerly climbed to the deck.

"I did it!" I yelled to my parents. "I faced my fears and conquered them!"

They cheered and clapped and came towards me carrying a huge blue beach towel. Mom wrapped me in it and hugged me. Mama B gave me a high five. I felt fantastic!

# Chapter 15

## *A Full Heart*

At bedtime Mom would tuck me in.  First, she'd kiss me.

"I love you, Joshie, see you in the morning," she'd say.

Then we'd puff out one of our cheeks, and pop them against each other.  It was something that Mom and Grandpa did, so we did it too.

We'd make our hands into the sign language symbol for "I love you," and we'd touch fingers.  Finally, we'd blow kisses to each other and pretend to catch them from the air.

One of us would say, "See you tomorrow!"

The other one would answer, "You've got a date."

Sometimes we'd just keep doing that over and over again.  I liked it when Mom would put me to bed and we'd finish our whole routine.  Then I'd say, "Would you rock me for a little while?"

She always did.  Then we'd get to go through our good night routine all over again.

Another fun thing that we liked to do was give each other "Blurbles."  That's our family name for a "Raspberry."  Mom gave me blurbles by putting her mouth on my bare belly or neck and blowing hard.  It tickles and makes a funny sound.  Blurbles always made me laugh!

Mom and I lived in her house for about six months.  Then she sold it and we moved into a bigger house that she and Mama B bought together.  The first night that we stayed in our new home, my bed had already been set up in my new room.  I noticed it had very big windows, and that there were no curtains on them yet.

"Ok, Honey, it's time for bed," Mom said.  "Hit the bathroom and brush your teeth, please.  Your bed is all ready for you."

"Mom, I don't want to sleep in that room without curtains," I told her.  "The windows are too big and it's too dark outside."

"You're right, Honey.  I'm sorry that we didn't think of that.  We'll just take a bunch of pillows and blankets, and make you a temporary bed in the guest bedroom. That room already has curtains. Do you think that will work for one night?"

"I never knew anybody wanted to take such good care of me like that," I told my mother, and meant it too.

"So am I 'dopted yet?" I asked.

"Well, not officially," Mom answered, "but in my heart you're already my son."

"Well, then, when are you going to 'dopt me?"

"Next weekend we're having your Naming Ceremony," Mom said. "On Monday, we'll go to the courthouse and talk with the judge."

"Then will I be yours forever?"

"You're already mine forever, Josh, but yes, the judge will legally make you mine."

It was the weekend just before our adoption became final. My parents had invited Mom's parents, Grandma and Grandpa, and mom's sister, Aunt Julie, to my Naming Ceremony.

Mama B's sister, Aunt Lynette, drove all the way from California to attend. LaTisha and her family came, and a few of my parents' closest friends.

A minister performed the Ceremony in our back yard. Mom had written the words just for me. It had special messages about new beginnings and my being part of this forever family. We had music, and it ended with singing.

Mom had one thing to say during the whole thing. The minister asked her, "Jamie, what name do you give your son?"

"Joshua Radford Carson," she said with a quivering voice and tears running down her cheeks.

Mom had decided to keep my old last name, and make it my new middle name. That's because I had already been Joshua Radford for nine years. Mom added her last name to the end of my old name.

At one point Mama B, Mom, and I gave each other jewelry pins to wear. The pins were little hands forming 'I love you' in sign language.

We had given the guests the words to "Joshua's Song." We ended by singing my words to the tune of "Barney's Song" from the kids' television show about the purple dinosaur.

"I love you, you love me, we're the perfect family, with Mom, Mama B, and Joshua too, happy Naming Day to you!"

We ate Cookies-n-Cream ice cream, and German Chocolate cake. Brooke took a lot of pictures. It was a great celebration.

My adoption became official the next day.

Being adopted is a really big deal. We got dressed up to go to court and appear in front of the judge. I like to get spiffed up, so I wore a suit and a tie. We all stood at attention when the judge entered the room.

"You may be seated," I heard somebody say.

"We have an adoption petition from Jamie Carson requesting to formalize her adoption of Joshua Radford," the judge began. "Are all parties present?"

"Yes, your Honor," Mom said.

"And are you Jamie Carson? Is this Joshua?" he asked and we answered.

"I'm assuming, by the tears running down your cheeks that you would like for me to grant this petition. Is that correct, Ms. Carson?"

"Yes, please, your Honor," she said, nodding her head and trying not to cry.

Mom explained happy tears to me a long time ago. She said, "Josh, sometimes my heart is so happy and full of so much love, that it makes tears overflow and spill out of my eyes. Those are my happy tears, and it's very good when I cry those tears."

Mom had cried happy tears on my "Naming Day," and now she was doing it again on our official adoption day. Mom must have been really happy about my adoption.

"Joshua, do you want Jamie Carson to be your forever mom?" I quickly nodded and quietly whispered, "Yes, please and thank you."

The judge smiled and said, "OK, then. I hereby legally declare you to be Mother and Son from this day forth. That entitles you to all of the rights and responsibilities, as if you were related via a natural birth."

Everyone cheered, cried, and hugged. We had our picture taken with the judge. Afterwards, Mom, Brooke, Aunt Lynette, and I went out to celebrate at my favorite restaurant. We each had my favorite food – pancakes.

"Josh, shall we go to your school and share the news with your classmates and teacher?" Mom asked.

"Yeah, that'd be tight!" I answered excitedly.

After a short drive in the car, we arrived at my school. Mom and I smiled as we walked in the classroom door holding hands. My teacher, Mrs. Jones, stopped writing on the blackboard, and everyone turned to look at us.

"I have an announcement to make," I told my classmates.

I walked up to the black board and picked up a piece of chalk. Very carefully, I printed this on the board: "My name is Joshua Radford Carson."

I turned to face the class and gave them a smile with a whole lot of teeth showing.

"Today, Joshua was adopted," Mrs. Jones said. "He and his mom became a forever family."

Mrs. Jones hugged me and then she hugged my mother. Everyone cheered.

I was happy and I knew Mom was too. That's because happy tears spilled out of her eyes. A couple of them landed on the back of my head, on my angel kiss. And that's how I started my life; as part of my forever family.

Mom says that my future is bright and that I have a lot to offer the world. I'm really happy about being 'dopted and excited about my new life.

I don't know if it's true that I'm lucky like a cat with nine lives. But I do know this, my name is Joshua Radford Carson, and I will survive.

# *The End*

# Resources

## Fetal Alcohol Spectrum Disorder (FASD)

National Organization on Fetal Alcohol Syndrome
www.nofas.org

FASD State Resource Directory
www.nofas.org/resource/directory

Available Assistance for Individuals with Disabilities
www.nofas.org/living

Community Resources & Family Support Groups
www.nofas.org/resource/results.aspx

Fetal Alcohol Syndrome Community Resource Center
Teresa Kellerman, Director
7725 E 33$^{rd}$ St
Tucson, AZ 85710
520-296-9172
www.come-over.to/FAS/Citizen
www.FASSTARS.com

"Iceberg" On-line Newsletter
www.fasiceberg.org

ADHD/ADD is often diagnosed with FASD
www.chadd.org

Support networks in each state for families, children, and
adults with special needs.
Judd103w@wonder.em.cdc.gov

The ARC has materials about Fetal Alcohol Syndrome.
www.thearc.org

FASD Center for Excellence
http://fasdcenter.samhsa.gov

This ARCH website helps families by listing various options for disabled and children in all 50 states.
www.respitelocator.org/index.htm

Parent support groups in multiple states
http://depts.washington.edu/fadu/Support.Groups.US.html

Parent support groups in Canada
http://depts.washington.edu/fadu/Support.Groups.CA.html

Directory: Charting the Future: Resource Directory for the Diagnosis, Prevention, and Treatment of Fetal Alcohol Syndrome; Barbara A Morse and Corinne Barnwell, Editors, 2000.

Fetal Alcohol Syndrome Diagnostic & Prevention Network
University of Washington
Seattle, WA

University of Washington Fetal Alcohol Drug Unit
180 Nickerson St, Suite 309
Seattle, WA 98109
206-543-7155
fadu@u.washington.edu
http://depts.washington.edu/fadu/

# ADOPTION

North American council on Adoptable Children has information on adoption subsidies, newsletters.
www.nacac.org

National Resource Center for Special Needs Adoption offers training and adoption support to families, newsletter.
www.spaulding.org

Parent Network for the Post-Institutionalized Child provides technical assistance for adoptions of children from hospitals and orphanages in other countries.
www.pnpic.org

National Adoption Center
www.adopt.org

Rainbow Kids, Adoption Information, Support, Photolistings
www.RainbowKids.com

Adoption Publishing Company, EMK Press, Publisher of books on adoption
www.emkpress.com

Tapestry Books
www.tapestrybooks.com

Adoption Shop
www.adoptionshop.com

Adoptive Families
www.adoptivefamilies.com

Come Unity
www.comeunity.com
Adoption Week e-magazine
http://e-magazine.adoption.com/

# Same Sex Parents

Family Pride
http://familypride.ecrater.com
www.familypride.org

Rainbow Families
www.rainbowfamilies.org

Human Rights Campaign (HRC)
www.hrc.org/familynet

www.proudparenting.com

www.gayparenting.com

www.andbabymagazine.com

# Meet the Author

## Jan Crossen, B.S., M.S.A.

Jan's interest in the welfare of children began years ago. As a high school teacher and coach, Jan was a mentor to many of her players. She has been a sponsor of children living in developing countries, and served as a court appointed surrogate parent for two young siblings in the Arizona foster care system.

Jan has always dreamed of creating her family through adoption. Her vision became a reality in 1999, when she adopted her son, Joshua. The three books in the *9 Lives* series were inspired by their lives together.

Jan would love to hear from you and may be contacted via:
- e-mail at info@jancrossen.com
- her website at www.jancrossen.com
- or through the United States Postal Service:

> Jan Crossen
> PO Box 915
> Lopez Island, WA 98261

# *9 Lives...*

## A three book series for:
- Older children, teens, and adults with lower reading abilities.
- Older children, teens, and adults with FASD.
- Foster & adopted children & teens.
- Children in interracial families.
- Children with same sex parents.
- Birth & adoptive parents.
- Healthcare & social workers.
- Counselors, therapists, & educators.
- Anyone who drinks alcohol or hopes to one day be a parent

## Joshua's story continues in Books 2 & 3 of the *9 Lives* Series

### Book 2: *9 Lives, Cat Tales*
Josh tells the story of his elementary school years when his behavioral problems began to emerge. He shares his interests in various activities, and visits a ranch for special animals and people. Josh meets the son of a famous African American Civil Rights leader, and makes an unusual Christmas wish.

### Book 3: *9 Lives, Full Circle*
The middle and high school years were difficult for Joshua. Like most teens, he struggles with his identity. He is handsome and has a normal IQ, yet he has social, academic, and behavioral issues that are hard to explain. These problems lead him down the wrong paths. He reunites with a birth family member, and realizes that he has an invisible disability. Josh must find a way to manage his handicap and achieve his dreams.

Printed in the United States
211968BV00001B/16/A

9 780979 398193